epic! originals

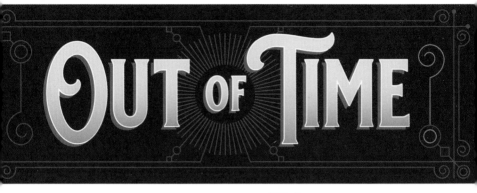

OUT OF TIME

LOST ON THE TITANIC

RMS TITANIC

LIVERPOOL

JESSICA RINKER

ILLUSTRATED BY BETHANY STANCLIFFE

Andrews McMeel
PUBLISHING®

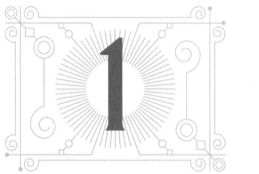

SATURDAY STRANGER

The last thing Allie and Vic Taylor wanted to do on a Saturday morning was clean. But they helped their parents in their shop anyway, just like they did every weekend. The Out of Time Antiques store on the corner of Third and Spruce in Philadelphia was the family business, and the whole family kept it running.

Allie polished a silver tea set while Vic dusted off an old violin. Their black-and-white puppy, Luna, who was very good for petting but not so good at fetching, walked all around the store. She wound around their legs and under the table and licked Allie's feet.

Allie laughed, while keeping her eyes on the little silver cup in her hands as she cleaned it. Mom had warned her to be careful with this set. Mom was hoping to find the teapot to go with it, but Allie hadn't found it in the pile of stuff yet. While she worked, Luna's sweet brown eyes and wiggly tail were begging Allie to take her out.

"Vic, can you take Luna for her walk?" Allie asked. As much as she loved Luna, she had been the one to take her out the last three times, and they were supposed to take turns.

"You take her. I'm doing an important job and can't be interrupted," said Vic.

Allie sighed and set down the cup. Big brothers were so bossy. Even when they were only one year older. Allie reached for Luna's leash, but just as she did, the little bell on the door chimed. A

HAVE YOU HEARD ABOUT EPIC! YET?

We're the largest digital library for kids, used by millions in homes and schools around the world. We love stories so much that we're now creating our own!

With the help of some of the best writers and illustrators in the world, we create the wildest adventures we can think of. Like a mermaid and narwhal who solve mysteries. Or a pet made out of slime.

We hope you have as much fun reading our books as we had making them!

customer? They hadn't had a customer all week!

But it was only Vic's best friend, Max.

"Hi, Vic," Max said. "Want to go to the park?"

"He can't," said Allie. "He's doing a very important job and can't be interrupted."

Vic crossed his arms and shook his head. Allie gave him a sweet smile. Luna barked at them both. Max laughed.

"Whose side are you on?" Vic asked Max.

"Luna's," he said, grinning. Max sat on the floor and patted Luna to settle her down. "What's the important job?"

"Mom had a doctor appointment and Dad had to run to the store for parts for our furnace. It stopped working again last night," Vic said.

"So we're helping them clean up their latest load of . . ." Allie waved her hand toward the table overflowing with objects of all sizes and colors.

"Junk?" Max asked.

"Don't let them hear you say that," Vic said.

"They're hoping something in here will be worth a lot of money," Allie said. She wasn't sure how an old bowl or teapot could be worth enough to replace

their furnace or take care of any other problem in their building, which always seemed to have problems. But she hoped her parents were right. The last thing she wanted to do was move out of their home, which was right above the shop. She'd lived there her whole life, and she loved walking to school and the park and the sandwich shop around the corner. Allie couldn't imagine ever living anywhere else, but she'd overheard her parents many times talking about how hard it was to afford living there. She'd do anything she could to help, even Saturday morning chores.

"I'll help," Max offered, giving Luna one last belly rub. "It'll get done quicker, and then we can all go to the park."

Vic handed Max a rag and some polish. "If you say so."

Luna lay down in a huff under the table. "Sorry, girl," Allie said. "We'll go out soon, I promise."

Just as they got back to work, the bell on the door chimed again. This time it was a real customer! Luna barked and barked—it had been a long time since a stranger had walked through the door. Vic held her collar so she wouldn't jump on the only customer they'd had in days.

The woman was tall and had long brown hair done up in a style unlike anything Allie had ever seen before. She wore a purple dress, a green cloak, and tall black boots, and she had a red bag strapped around her waist. But what really stood out were her honey-colored eyes. Something about the woman was familiar, but Allie couldn't quite figure out what.

"Can we help you?" Allie asked.

"I'm looking for Allison and Victor Taylor," the woman said. She had an accent that none of the kids recognized. "Do you know them?"

"Uh . . . I'm Victor, but everyone

calls me Vic. And this is my sister, Allie. Do you mean you want to talk to our parents?"

"No," the woman said. A large smile spread across her face. "I came to see you two. And you." She pointed at Max.

"Me?" Max said. "Why me?"

"Because this involves all three of you. And your futures. My name is Juniper. I have something important to give you . . ." But before she could finish explaining, Luna began barking and lunging at her again.

"Luna, quiet," Vic said. "Sorry, she's not usually like this." He tried to hold on to her, but Luna pulled away from Vic's hands and jumped right up on the woman, nearly knocking her over.

Something round and glowing fell from the woman's hands with a loud thunk. It jingled as it rolled across the floor. All three kids grabbed for it, but no one could move quicker than Luna.

She gobbled up the glowing ball in one gulp.

THE INFINITY SPINNER

Luna!" Vic yelled. "No!"

"It's too late," Allie said. She tried to look in Luna's mouth. "She swallowed it!"

"Hey, at least Luna fetched," said Max.

"Fetching usually involves bringing

the ball back," Juniper said. Allie couldn't tell if she was angry or making a joke. But she looked worried.

"Excuse me, ma'am, but what was that thing?" asked Allie. She imagined all kinds of bad things happening to Luna. "It was glowing. It's not going to explode, is it?" She wrapped her arms around Luna.

"No, no, no," Juniper sighed as if she saw this sort of thing every day. "Nothing of the sort. Luna will be just fine."

"I don't think it's good for her to swallow anything whole," Vic said. "We should probably take her to the V-E-T."

He had to spell it because Luna hated going to the veterinarian, and she'd run and hide if she heard him say the word out loud.

"Good idea," said Juniper. "Because we need that Infinity Spinner back. The sooner the better. I have a lot to teach you."

Allie looked at Vic, who looked at Max. "What's an Infinity Spinner?" Max asked.

"And will it do something bad to Luna?" Allie asked.

"It won't do anything. At least

not on its own. It's kind of like a GPS that works in time and space," Juniper said. "But it can't fall into the wrong hands." She looked at Luna. "Or stomachs."

Juniper must have been able to tell that Allie wasn't believing any of this, because she said, "I know it sounds crazy, but your future depends on us getting that Spinner back."

"What is that supposed to mean?" Vic asked.

"I will explain everything once the vet—"

"Shhh!" Vic said. "She knows that word!" He covered Luna's ears with his hands.

"I'll explain everything once the V-E-T helps Luna. I promise. But we don't have a lot of time to waste," said Juniper.

Allie ran over to her parents' desk and found the vet's number. Her hands were shaking, so Vic took the phone and made the call. When he told them it was an emergency, Allie's heart felt like it was beating extra hard. If only she'd taken Luna out earlier, none of this would have happened. Luna was only a puppy. She didn't know any better.

"Everything will be okay." Max brought the leash to Allie.

Allie attached it to Luna's collar, and all five of them left the little shop on the corner. "We walk to the V-E-T all the time," Allie told Juniper. "She gets into a lot of trouble."

Juniper laughed. "I know."

Max raised his eyebrows at Allie. She shrugged. Maybe Juniper had seen them walking to the vet before. She didn't care. She just wanted Luna to be safe.

Luna seemed to be feeling fine. But when they got closer to the vet, the dog realized where they were going. She began bouncing around and barking. Luna pulled so hard, she nearly dragged

Allie off the sidewalk. Juniper tried to help, but before she could, Luna twisted just right and slipped out of her collar. She ran down the sidewalk and away from the vet, dashing between people as she went.

"LUNA!" All three kids yelled and chased after her. Juniper yelled for them to wait for her, but they kept going. They had to stop Luna from running

away or, worse, running into traffic!

Max was the fastest, sprinting ahead of Vic and Allie. Luna looked back at them twice, but she just kept running. It looked like she was even smiling at them, enjoying the chase.

"LUNA!" Allie pretended she had something in her hand. "Treat!"

"Genius," Max said.

Luna stopped running. She turned

to them. She sniffed the sidewalk. She sniffed a man's shoe. The man grabbed at Luna. Relieved that someone had stopped to help, all three kids ran toward him. But he had a smile on his face that wasn't entirely friendly. And he was wearing a long cloak like Juniper's, only it looked like it was made out of something like tinfoil, which didn't make any sense in the middle of the afternoon. Actually, it didn't make any sense at any time.

Allie did not like the look on his face, and she wanted her puppy back.

"No!" Juniper yelled when she saw him, startling everyone. The man let go of Luna and ran. Luna went right on sniffing.

"Who was that?" Vic asked.

"Just get the dog," Juniper yelled. "Fast!"

Then Luna started chasing her tail.

"What in the world is she doing?" Allie asked.

"I think she forgot about the V-E-T," Max said.

"Now's our chance to catch her," Allie said.

They snuck up on Luna as she spun five times, happily playing with her own tail like it was the very first time she'd seen it. But just as Vic was about to grab her, they were blinded by a flash of light. Then the three of them were lifted off their feet, and everything seemed to spin.

The last thing Allie heard was Juniper yelling, "WAIT!"

When the flash of light was gone
and the spinning stopped, Allie rubbed
her eyes.

They were no longer standing on a
sidewalk in the city.

They were in the middle of the
ocean, on the deck of a very large ship.

ALL ABOARD

*A*llie grabbed the railing. Luna was nowhere in sight. Allie tried not to panic, but Luna was still so young. How would she know what to do on a ship? How would *they* know what to do on a ship? This had to be some kind of strange dream!

Allie stared at the enormous stacks above them. Max leaned over the railing and peered at the raging waves beneath the ship. The air was very cold and damp. It made Allie's nose and throat hurt a little.

Max was the first to speak. "What. Just. Happened?"

"I'm not sure," said Vic. "But I think we're on an ocean liner. One of those huge ships that used to carry people across the Atlantic."

"It looks like the Titanic," Allie whispered. Although she was worried about Luna, history was Allie's favorite subject and she couldn't help but be amazed at what she saw. She'd learned about the Titanic in school, and this ship looked like a page right out of her textbook. But there was no way they could be standing on the deck of a ship that had sunk more than 100 years ago!

"Yes," Vic said. "Exactly like the Titanic." But he looked like he didn't believe what he was saying. He also looked a little scared. That worried Allie. Vic was never afraid of anything.

"That's not possible," Max said as a man wearing a top hat and a long coat came toward them, looking at the three of them like they were creatures from another planet. As the man walked past, Max reached up and tapped the man's hat.

"Max!" Allie grabbed his arm.

Fortunately, the well-dressed man kept walking.

"I know it's not possible. But we're looking at it!" Vic said. "One second you were trying to catch Luna, and the next

we're standing here."

"Her spinning must have sent us here," Allie said. "Her spinning and that Spinner stuck inside her." Allie thought about poor Luna lost on this huge ship all by herself. The poor pup had never even seen the ocean.

"Just like Juniper said: 'A GPS for time and space,'" Max said. "What if she was telling the truth? What if it turned Luna into a . . . portal of some sort?"

"Where *is* Luna?" Allie asked. She looked down the deck in both directions and all she saw were people in the distance. The ship was so big, it was like looking down several city blocks.

"It's freezing. We have to find her and get home!"

"How do you suppose we do that?" Max asked. "Swim?"

Allie hugged herself to keep warm. "If we're right and Luna's a portal and chasing her tail got us here, chasing her tail again has to get us back. Right?"

Neither of the boys answered.

They walked the deck for a while, looking for their black-and-white dog. They passed lifeboats hanging above the deck and large red-and-white flotation rings. Everywhere they looked, there were doors and passageways leading off of the deck. Allie might have actually enjoyed exploring the massive ship if she weren't so worried about Luna. And getting home.

Every once in a while, they called Luna's name. But there was no sign of her, and Allie wasn't sure if Luna would even be able to hear them over the crashing waves and groaning ship engines. She also wondered if maybe Luna hadn't made it to the ship in the first place. Maybe she'd spun off somewhere else.

Maybe the three of them were stuck there.

If Vic was right and this was the Titanic, they were in very big trouble.

As they turned the corner near the front of the ship, a man dressed in a white cap and a black jacket with lots of buttons stopped them. Allie knew he had to be part of the crew. His name tag said Officer Lowe.

"What are you kids doing up here?" Officer Lowe asked. He had a British accent. His nose was red from the cold. "Get back to your quarters. This section is for first-class passengers only."

The officer stood still, blocking their way. Allie saw a few people behind him: women dressed in full, ruffled gowns and men dressed all in black. No one was wearing jeans or sweatshirts, like

she and the boys were. Everyone looked elegant and old-fashioned, like the people in the antique photographs her parents never sold.

But there was still no sign of Luna.

"Sir?" Allie asked. "What is the name of this ship?"

Officer Lowe looked at her like she was trying to start trouble. "Little lady, unless you are a stowaway, you know perfectly well you're aboard the unsinkable Titanic. Now off with you. Get back to third class, where you and these other ruffians belong!"

"Yes, sir," Vic said, trying to pull his sister and best friend along. "We're

leaving. Sorry to bother you." Vic, Allie,
and Max turned and quickly walked
back in the direction they'd come from.

"Well, I think now we know for sure
what the Infinity Spinner does," Vic

said. He stopped walking and pointed to one of the flotation rings.

"What?" asked Max. But Allie already saw what Vic was pointing at.

Printed on the side was RMS TITANIC.

There was no doubt now. Juniper's Infinity Spinner had made them travel through time and space. And it had landed them on the deck of the Titanic.

"This is not good," Max said, shaking his head. "Not good at all. Way worse than the V-E-T."

"We've got to find Luna. And fast," Allie said.

"This ship is enormous," Vic said. "Where do we start?"

"If I know anything about Luna," said Max, "it's that she loves to eat."

Allie nodded. "Yes! The kitchen. We have to find the kitchen. I think it's called a galley, on a ship." And on a ship this big, Allie thought, there were probably several. She had learned that the Titanic had many levels of living quarters, and she guessed that each one probably had its own galley. Any one of them would be Luna's personal puppy paradise.

"We have to start somewhere," she said, pushing open a door that led into a long, bright, warm passageway. "Let's follow our noses."

RUTH

*A*llie, Vic, and Max walked as confidently as they could through the colorful corridors of the ship, trying to pretend they belonged there. They passed a family dressed like the other people Allie had seen, and they saw more crew members. No one questioned

why the three kids were there, but they got a lot of funny looks. Allie even saw one little boy move closer to his parents as they passed, like he was afraid of them. After walking down what felt like the world's longest hallway, Allie began to smell something delicious, just as she'd hoped she would.

"I smell ham," she whispered to the boys. "And . . . cinnamon apples! You know Luna would love that."

"Follow the smell," Max said, raising his fist. "Find the dog!"

They turned the corner, and the delicious sweet-and-savory odor grew stronger. Allie figured the set of double doors right ahead of them would lead to a galley, but instead of seeing Luna waiting outside the doors, like Allie had hoped, she saw a young girl with a huge bow in her hair. The girl was trying to peek through one of the little round windows.

"That's not Luna," Vic said.

"Who's Luna?" the girl asked, spinning around. Her dress twirled as she turned to face them. "Oh!" She

looked the three of them up and down and tried to stop herself from laughing.

"Luna's our puppy. She's lost somewhere on the ship," Allie explained, suddenly feeling even more out of place in her jeans and sneakers. "We were hoping she'd followed the delicious smells coming from the galley."

Allie introduced herself and the boys to the girl. The girl replied, "I'm Ruth. I followed those smells, too. Sometimes the waitstaff sneaks me a snack." She grinned and gave them a funny look. "Where are you three from?"

"Philadelphia, Pennsylvania," Max answered.

"What room are you in?"

"Uhh . . ." Vic looked around the passageway for a hint.

But before he had to come up with an answer, Ruth said, "I'm in second class with my mother and brother, who's sick. We're taking him to America to see a good doctor, but my mother's real nervous about this ship, so I have to sneak out to explore. My father will be coming later, on another boat."

Allie knew the Titanic had three classes. The more money a passenger had paid for their ticket, the higher up on the ship they got to stay. And the higher up they were, the more likely

WHITE STAR LINE.

First Class Passenger Ticket per Steamship *Titanic* 10/4 1912

they were to get off the ship before it sank. But most people didn't survive the sinking. The more she thought about it, the more nervous Allie felt.

Just as she was starting to think that they should warn Ruth about what was going to happen, the galley doors swung open. A waiter dressed all in white and carrying a large tray full of plates of ham, bread, and baked apples came out, looking surprised to see the four of them standing there.

"Little lady, I told you—no more sneaking up here," he said to Ruth. "You're going to get both of us in trouble, especially if you start bringing friends."

"They belong here. They're first class," Ruth said, crossing her arms. The waiter looked at Allie, Vic, and Max, shook his head, and laughed.

"Doubtful," he said, but he handed them each a good-size piece of ham and a slice of bread and quickly went on his way.

"What, no apples?" Max asked, his mouth full of food.

"Are you brothers and sister?" Ruth asked as she chewed.

"Max is our friend," said Allie.

"Max is *my* friend." Vic put his arm around Max.

Ruth put her arm around Allie. "Then you're *my* friend."

"Pretty sure we can all be friends, guys." Max swallowed his last bite and wiped his hands on his pants. Then he looked at Ruth and seemed worried. "Well, sort of."

Allie knew that Max was thinking the same thing she was: everyone on this ship was in danger, and they had no idea. But it was hard to focus on that with her stomach growling so loudly. She hadn't realized how hungry she

was until she had the warm bread in her hands. Time traveling must make you hungry, she thought. However, even though it tasted delicious and she wanted to savor every last bite, she knew it would be the perfect bait to catch Luna with. The boys and Ruth ate all of theirs, but Allie tucked half of hers into her pocket.

"You can get all the food you want up in first class," Ruth said. "You don't have to save it."

"It's a treat for Luna. We have to find her, or we're never going to get home," Allie said. She thought they should warn Ruth before they went on their way to look for Luna, or Ruth would never get home, either.

"There's something we should tell you," said Allie. "The Titanic . . ."

"Wait!" Vic shouted, making Allie jump. "Don't."

"Why not?"

"Because . . . haven't you ever heard how it's bad to try to change history? It could have ripple effects all through time that we don't even know about."

"Yeah, but the ripples might be good in this case!" said Allie.

"What on earth are you all talking about?" Ruth asked. "What ripples?"

"We'll explain later," Vic said. "Let's go look for Luna." Allie was angry at her brother for not letting her tell Ruth what would happen to the Titanic, but she thought Vic might be right about the ripple effects. Still, when they looked at each other, Allie knew they were all wondering the same thing: Would Ruth ever make it to America?

DOGGONE AGAIN

Tell me what Luna looks like," Ruth said, "and I'll help you find her."

"Black and white, four legs, and a tail," Vic said.

Allie rolled her eyes. He always thought he was so funny. "She's all that and super soft, with big, beautiful brown eyes, and she loves to run and chase her tail . . ."

"You can say that again," Max said. "She has a tiny bit of white at the very end of her tail, like a paintbrush dipped in paint. Also, she loves shoes." He lifted up his sneaker and showed Ruth his chewed-up laces.

"All right!" Ruth said. "Let's find this puppy!"

Allie still wanted to warn Ruth about the disaster that was coming, especially now that she was going to help them find Luna. Even though she agreed with Vic for now, she still planned to let Ruth know she was in danger before they went home. But they couldn't get home without Luna.

Ruth knew the ship so well, she had them running through beautiful ballrooms, decadent dining halls, art galleries, libraries, and even a room with a swimming pool! They entered an ornate dining room, where most of the people ignored them as they squeezed past their conversations and dinner parties.

Everywhere the kids looked, there were brightly polished things. Allie had never seen so many shiny things— silverware, vases, even the walls themselves.

"Mom and Dad would go crazy here," Vic said as they examined shelves of plates and bowls in every color.

"And none of it even has to be dusted," said Max, running his finger over a silver teapot that looked awfully familiar to Allie. In fact, it looked like it matched the tea set she'd been polishing that morning. It must have been the missing teapot! Her mom would be so excited! Allie reached out to pick it up when someone shouted behind them.

"Do NOT touch the fine silver!"

The kids all swung around to see a woman wearing an enormous feathered hat and a ruffled lace dress. "What are you staring at?" she asked. "You don't even belong in the dining room, you hooligans. What kind of parents let their children run all over the place dressed in . . . well, whatever it is you're wearing?"

"Sorry, ma'am," Ruth said. "We're trying to find my friends' lost dog."

"Of course you are," the woman said. "By any chance, is this dog black with white paws?"

"Yes!" Allie said. "Have you seen her?"

"Does this dog like to steal things?"

"That's Luna," Allie said.

"What did she steal this time?" Vic asked.

"Whatever it was, I hope she didn't eat it," Max said.

The woman held up a white glove. "The match to this. I was lounging on the top deck when a furry blur ran through and knocked over everyone's glasses with her tail. She ran up to me and looked me right in the eye, as if she were saying, 'Hello there, Miss Molly

Brown. I'm going to steal your glove now.' And that's exactly what she did. Snatched it right off my lap."

"That's definitely Luna," Allie said. "She's really a very friendly dog."

"She mostly likes to be chased," Max added.

"Yes, well, it worked," Molly Brown said. "I tried to catch her, but she was too fast. She likes to chase her tail a lot, too."

"Oh no," Allie said. "What if she spun in circles again and left us here?"

"How could she leave?" Ruth asked. "We're in the middle of the ocean. I'm sure she's around here somewhere.

Don't worry, we'll find her."

"I hope you're right," Max said. "Because if not, we're all doomed."

Vic elbowed Max in the arm. "Shhh! I don't think it's a good idea to say anything. Remember?"

"I don't know, Vic. The more I think about it, wouldn't it be a good thing?" Max whispered. "Save everyone on the Titanic? Save ourselves, if we can't find Luna?"

"Hasn't anyone ever told you that whispering is rude? And save us from what?" Molly Brown asked. "The likes of you four?" She laughed and laughed as though this were the funniest joke

anyone had ever told.

"Come on, guys," Allie said. "We're running out of time."

She grabbed Ruth by the sleeve and ran back into the passageway. Behind her, Molly Brown called out, "Bring me back my glove when you find her! I'll be reading on the upper deck."

"Yes, ma'am!" Ruth called out. "I like that lady," she said. "But why do Vic and Max think they have to save everyone on the Titanic?"

"We'll explain later," Allie said. "I promise." She felt horrible about not telling her new friend the truth.

The boys joined them in the passageway, and the four of them tried to decide where to look next. They didn't have to think for too long because right up ahead, they saw a dark blur dash out of one room and into the next. Luna!

"There she is!" Allie shouted. As they ran toward the room, they saw someone else come out and run after Luna, too.

It was a woman dressed in purple and green, with a red bag around her waist.

OUT OF TIME

It's the lady from the store!" Max shouted. They watched as Juniper swished around a corner and was gone.

"Hurry up!" cried Allie. "She's going to get to Luna before we do. We have to tell her we're here!" Allie grabbed Max and pulled him down the passageway with her. Ruth and Vic ran behind them.

"How is this even possible?" Vic yelled as they ran. "We left that lady on the sidewalk in Philadelphia! Didn't we? I'm so confused!"

"How did you get on the ship, anyway? We left from England, not Philadelphia." Ruth seemed confused, but they could tell by her grin that she was enjoying the crazy adventure she'd gotten pulled into.

None of them answered her, but she still followed them as they ran down the hall, following flashes of the woman's dress—around corners, through a dining hall and music room, and then through a set of doors that opened to reveal a huge staircase that wrapped around the room. Allie, Vic, and Max all gasped. Ruth led them up the steps, squeezing past couples coming down, so they could look over the balcony. There was a beautiful dome window and a gigantic chandelier hanging above them. Allie thought it looked like something that belonged in a palace.

Ruth said, "Grand, isn't it?"

Down below, Luna wagged her tail at the woman in purple and green, who was crouched down in front of her. Juniper was saying something to Luna that they couldn't hear. Allie noticed

that she had another one of those glowing balls in her hand, just like the one Luna had swallowed, only this one was green. A second Infinity Spinner! Allie nudged Max and pointed. Max's eyes widened, and he leaned over the railing.

"Hey, lady!" he shouted. Everyone around them stopped talking.

Juniper startled and rose to her feet, but she held tightly on to Luna. "You three made it here after all." She grinned. Allie couldn't figure out what she was so happy about. *Here* was not exactly a great place to be! But at least Luna hadn't spun off without them. She must not have chased her tail enough to go anywhere else. They all ran down to Luna.

Allie bent down and hugged her. "Don't ever run away again, sweet girl."

Luna licked Allie's cheek and nibbled her ear. It was her way of apologizing.

"No glove," Ruth said.

"She probably ate it," said Vic, as Allie slipped Luna's collar back on. "This dog probably has a whole department store in her stomach. I don't know how we will explain this one to the V-E-T." He turned to Juniper. "How exactly did we get here, anyway?"

"Did you send us away on purpose?" asked Max.

"Will the Spinner still work to get us home?" asked Allie.

Luna barked.

"WHAT IS GOING ON?" Ruth shouted over all of them. Several people stopped in their tracks to see what the fuss was all about, and Juniper ushered them to the edge of the room so they wouldn't attract any more attention.

"Listen, all of you, I don't have enough time to explain everything," Juniper started, but she was interrupted by a woman shouting.

"Ruthie Elizabeth Becker! I've been

looking everywhere for you, young lady, and you are not supposed to be up here. Your brother is in the cabin waiting, and you know how I feel about this rickety . . . boat! What possessed you to run off like this? And who are these awful children?" She eyed Vic's sweatshirt like it was on fire and quickly pulled Ruth to her side.

At that, Juniper looked Allie, Vic, and Max right in the eyes. "I can't stay. There's someone I have to find before he finds you. Go get that silver teapot. Get your dog to spin five times. Get home." She looked worried for a moment, but then she put her hands on Allie's

shoulders and whispered, "I know you can do this. It's what you were born to do. Trust me." And then she ran up the stairs, spun around five times, and vanished.

Ruth's mother looked like she might faint.

"Please! Wait!" Allie yelled. But it was too late. Juniper was gone. Allie wanted to cry. Someone was after them, and Juniper left them behind?

Max squeezed Allie's hand. "It'll be okay," he said. "She's right. We've got Luna."

"But now we need a teapot?" Vic asked, scratching his head. "I don't get it."

Allie knew exactly which teapot they needed, although she didn't understand why. But before she could tell Vic, she noticed Ruth's mother quickly leading Ruth away.

"I didn't even say goodbye to my friends yet!" Ruth said.

"Too bad," her mother said. "We're

going back to our cabin right now."

Ruth waved as her mother guided her away. "It was nice to meet you. Glad you got your dog back! Maybe I'll see you in America!"

"Wait!" Allie called after Ruth, but Ruth's mother held up her hand to stop her. "That's enough, child," she said and whisked Ruth away. Allie felt sick to her stomach. They'd never had a chance to explain to Ruth what was going to happen to the Titanic. Now Allie really felt like crying, but she blinked back the tears as best she could. "What time is it?" she asked Vic, wiping her face dry.

"What does that matter? I don't

even know what day it is." Vic rubbed his face. He watched as Allie hooked the leash back onto Luna's collar, making sure it was tight enough that the puppy wouldn't slip out of it again. Luna licked Allie's hand.

"Is time even a thing anymore," asked Max, "if you're trapped in 1912?"

"The ship hits an iceberg late at

night—almost midnight, I think," Allie whispered. "I remember learning in class that so many people were already in bed when it happened that a lot of them never knew anything was wrong until it was too late. No one thought this ship could sink, even when it was in trouble. If we go after Ruth now, we can still warn her before it's too late."

"We don't even know what room she's in," said Vic.

"Well, then we can just knock on every door and warn everyone!" Allie said.

A giant clock chimed.

One, two, three, four, five, six, seven, eight, nine, ten, eleven.

"We have to move fast," Allie said, gripping Luna's leash tightly. "If tonight is the night the Titanic sinks, we're running out of time."

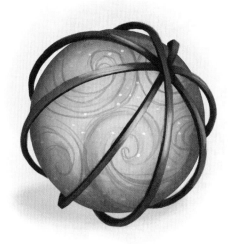

STOWAWAYS

$\mathcal{A}$llie, Vic, and Max tried to find their way to the second-class cabins, where they knew Ruth was staying with her family. Luna ran along beside them, happy to be back with her family. On the way, Allie slipped back into the dining room where they'd seen the silver teapot. The room was empty, and some of the tables were set for breakfast. She slid one of the tablecloths off a table, wrapped the teapot inside, and slung it over her shoulder.

"This is ridiculous," Vic said.

"I don't know," Max said. "I feel like

Juniper wouldn't tell us to get the teapot if it wasn't important."

"I don't like the idea of stealing, but all of this stuff will be at the bottom of the ocean soon," Allie said, shivering at the thought. "Now let's find Ruth."

But the ship was so large and there were so many rooms and staircases and doors that they quickly realized they'd never find Ruth in time.

"We need a better plan," said Max. Vic and Allie agreed. They were going to need to ask someone for help. The only person Allie could think of was Molly Brown.

"She could warn the crew," Allie

told the boys. "They'd listen to her before they'd listen to us. Plus, she said she'd be on the upper deck reading, so she should be easy to find."

"They're just going to think she's crazy. And she's going to think *we're* crazy," said Vic. "It's a dumb idea."

"You have a better one?" asked Allie.

"Yeah, as a matter of fact, I do! Get Luna to chase her tail right now so we can get off this ship before it sinks!"

"I don't care what you say—I'm not going home without warning Ruth!" Allie got up on tiptoe to try to make herself as tall as Vic. It didn't work.

"Okay, you two," Max said, gently pulling Allie and Vic away from each other. "Don't fight. It's not going to help. It's a good plan. And Allie's right—we have to try."

"What about the whole 'changing history' thing?" asked Vic.

"I think we should let it slide this one time," Max said. "Allie had a valid point. Maybe the ripple effects will be good."

"And *then* we get Luna to chase her tail?" Vic asked.

"Yes."

Together they ran back up the grand staircase and found their way to the upper deck. It was freezing outside now, and very dark. The wind nearly blew them over, and Allie wondered if Molly would even be out here anymore. Who could read in this wind?

But they made their way toward the front of the ship anyway, and there were people there in spite of the cold, tucked into little alcoves and protected from the wind. Bands played music. Waiters served drinks. And there, sitting under a wool blanket and reading a book by the glow of a lamp, was Molly Brown.

"Ah-ha! The little furball thief herself," she said when she saw Luna. "Did you bring back my glove?"

"No, ma'am," Allie said. "We looked,
but we couldn't find it. We're hoping
Luna didn't eat it."

"She's a regular garbage truck,"
Max said.

"Well, blast if I have any idea what you're talking about, son, but it's high time everyone gets to bed, I suppose."

"But we came to find you for a reason," Allie said. She cleared her throat. "There's something we need to tell you. We know something that you should know. That everyone on this ship should know, and we need your help to tell them."

"Well go ahead, child. Don't just stand there letting the words freeze in the air," Molly said. "Get to the point!"

"The Titanic's going to sink," Vic blurted out.

Molly looked serious for a moment, and then her face scrunched up really tight and she laughed and laughed. "Don't be ridiculous. Everyone knows this ship is unsinkable. You sure have big imaginations." She smiled and tousled Vic's hair. "Get yourselves back to your cabin before you freeze to death." Molly gathered up her things and headed inside. "The Titanic sink . . . oh my stars," she chuckled as she went.

"So much for that idea," said Allie.

She looked down at Luna, who was now lying on the ground, panting hard.

"You okay, girl?" Allie asked. "Vic, she doesn't look good."

"Of course she doesn't. She ate half of the ship today."

"We have to get her home."

"Yes, we do. And we have to get *us* home."

"Let's sneak into one of the rooms and try to get Luna to spin," Vic said.

"Okay." Allie got Luna to stand, and they made their way to the grand staircase once more, only to be stopped by a frowning crew member: Officer Lowe.

"You three again. Children are

not allowed on the deck after ten," he said.

"We're going back to our room now," said Vic.

"And what room is that?" Officer Lowe crossed his arms.

Vic blinked.

"Tickets?" he asked.

Vic blinked again.

"And what's this?" Officer Lowe grabbed the bundle slung over Allie's shoulder. No one knew what to say.

"That's what I thought—thieves and stowaways," he said, grabbing Vic's sweatshirt hood. "You're coming with me to see the master-at-arms."

"The who?" Vic asked.

"It's like the police on a ship," Allie whispered. She shivered.

This was not good at all.

ICEBERG, STRAIGHT AHEAD

The temperature seemed to be dropping by the second, so Allie was relieved when they finally got out of the night air. Allie looked over at Max as they followed behind Officer Lowe and Vic and Luna. She was hoping he'd have some kind of plan, but Max only shrugged. They couldn't run and leave Vic, and even if Vic got out of the man's grasp, they still needed the teapot.

Luna trotted next to them through the corridor but abruptly stopped when they turned a corner. A man in a strange metallic cloak stood in the middle of the passageway.

"Excuse me, sir." Officer Lowe tipped his hat. "Escorting these three to the master-at-arms."

"I can take them from here," the other man said, reaching for Luna's leash. Allie held it tight.

"And who are you?" Officer Lowe let go of Vic's hood and eyed the man in the

tinfoil cloak suspiciously. Vic took a few
steps back.

"My name is Atlas, and I'm
responsible for these three. Four, if you
count the furry one."

"No he's not!" Allie blurted out. "And you can't have our puppy!"

"Silly girl," Atlas laughed. "I don't want the puppy."

Officer Lowe's eyebrows pinched together as he tried to make sense of what was going on. "I think it best for the master-at-arms to sort this out," he told Atlas. He tried to get by, but Atlas wouldn't budge. He was a large man, and he took up most of the passageway just by standing in it. Plus light reflected off his weird cloak at all kinds of angles, making their eyes hurt.

Before either of the men could do anything, a massive jolt shook the entire ship, knocking them all to their knees. Everything shook, lights flickered on and off, and Officer Lowe dropped the bundled-up teapot.

"There's that iceberg!" Atlas said. "Right on time."

The shaking stopped, but Allie knew the real danger was coming. She reached down and grabbed the bundled teapot. "Let's go!" she yelled to Vic and Max.

They ran as fast as they could back in the direction they had come from, ignoring the shouts of both men behind them. People began pouring into the passageway to see what the commotion was. The crowd was hard to get through, but it helped them hide from Atlas and Officer Lowe. They ducked into a little sitting room and shut the door.

"Who *is* that guy?" Vic asked.

"Must be who Juniper was trying to find," Allie said.

Some of the lights flickered, and the entire ship seemed to groan and creak.

"We'd better make Luna spin right now or we really *are* going to have to swim home," Max said, trying to catch his breath.

"Luna, come on girl!" Allie said in the most cheerful voice she could, even though she did not feel the least bit cheerful. She playfully wagged Luna's tail. "Chase it! Go get it!"

"Come on, Luna," the boys said, gesturing in circles. "Around and around!"

Luna barked and jumped at all the excitement, but she didn't seem to understand what they were trying to get her to do. Vic spun in a circle. Max spun in a circle. Allie scratched Luna's back. "See? You have to spin in circles!"

The room shuddered.

"What's it gonna take to make this dog spin?" Vic nearly pulled his hair out.

Allie suddenly remembered. She

reached into her pocket and pulled out the chunk of bread she'd saved. It was squished, but Luna wouldn't care. Allie waved it in front of the puppy's face and led her in circles until finally Luna began to spin around.

"Faster, Luna!" they all shouted.

After five spins, there was a large flash of light. Just like before, their feet left the ground. When they landed, they were back on the sidewalk in Philadelphia.

It was sunny, and traffic was noisy.

It was as if they'd never even left.

Allie still had the teapot slung over her shoulder and the bread in her hand.

She bent down and hugged Luna. "You did it, girl! You saved us!" she said as she gave Luna her treat.

Vic and Max bent down to pet Luna, too.

"Keeping that bread was really smart, Allie," Vic said.

"And it's a good thing you knew so much about the Titanic," Max added.

"Thanks." Allie smiled.

Luna licked Allie's cheek. That was her way of asking, "Do you have any more bread?"

"All right. We can't waste any more time." Vic took Luna's leash. "We're going to the V-E-T right this minute!"

BACK TO NORMAL . . . ALMOST

Luna recovered from her ordeal quite well. The vet removed the Infinity Spinner and several other items, and Luna only had to rest for a few days. But her surgery was very expensive, so the Taylors had to return the furnace parts and use the money to pay the vet.

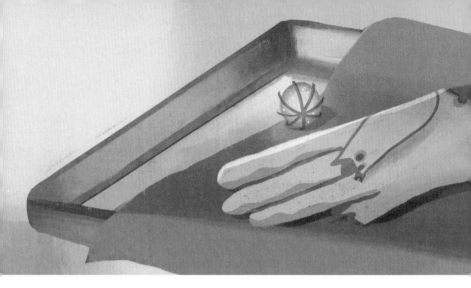

They were right back where they started, with no heat and no customers.

"Where did you say you found this little purple glowing ball?" their father asked Vic and Allie. He inspected it after the vet returned it to them.

"It was in the pile of things you left for us to clean," Allie said. She and Vic had decided to keep quiet about Juniper for now. They didn't know if they'd even

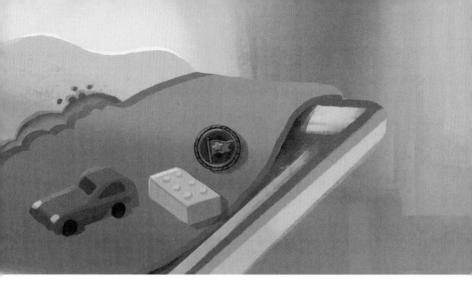

see her again. "Can we keep it?"

Mr. Taylor tossed it to Allie. "I guess. Doesn't look like it's worth anything. Just a toy."

Allie looked at Vic, who was thinking the same thing: If only their dad knew the truth.

Just then, the little bell on the door rang. Mr. Taylor looked up, hopeful. "Oh. It's you."

"Yeah—just me," Max said. "Sorry to disappoint."

"You are never a disappointment, Max," Mrs. Taylor said as she came into the room with polish and rags. "We're just hoping for customers, as always." She handed all three kids clean rags. "How about we get back to work?"

Then Mr. Taylor went to the basement to try and get the furnace running again, and Mrs. Taylor closed herself in the office to work on some bookkeeping for the store.

None of the kids were particularly excited about dusting and polishing, but they were happy to be home. Allie would take anything over being on the Titanic.

The first thing she'd done after getting home was to go online to look up Ruth and Molly. The Titanic still sank, but she was relieved to find that both Ruth's family and Molly Brown had gotten off the ship and lived long lives. So did Officer Lowe. Maybe Molly had believed them after all, or maybe they were all just lucky. Allie would never know the truth.

But she was still sad about all of the people who did not get off the ship, and she wondered what would have happened if they'd warned the crew to avoid the iceberg. It was one of the many things she wished she could ask Juniper. She also felt bad that her parents had to spend so much money at the V-E-T. Allie wished she could do something to change all of it.

"If only we knew how to make the Infinity Spinner take us to the exact time we wanted to go to," she said as they cleaned. "Then we could go back to last weekend and make sure Juniper told us everything before Luna swallowed the Spinner."

"I'm here to tell you everything now." The lady in purple and green with the honey-colored eyes had appeared right in the middle of the room.

"Juniper!"

"Thank goodness you all made it back," Juniper said. "I mean, I already knew you would. But thank goodness!" She bent down and patted Luna, too. "Glad to see you back in good health." Luna barked, but she didn't jump up.

"Are you going to tell us what's going on now?" Allie asked.

"I am." Juniper smiled. She pulled a thick, worn book from her bag. It said *Treasure Travelers* across the cover. "This is your guide. This is the reason I'm going to teach you how to use the Infinity Spinner. And the reason I exist at all."

"You exist because of a book?" Vic asked.

"I exist because our family has a very special place in history," Juniper said.

"Our family?" Max asked.

Juniper smiled and put her hands on Allie's and Max's shoulders. "Let's just say that, in the future, we're all related. But what you need to know now is that this book contains all the treasures lost throughout history, like the little silver teapot you already saved. It's up to you three to find them."

"Are you saying we're, like, time thieves?" Max asked. Allie didn't like the sound of that.

"No, no, nothing like that," Juniper laughed. "Just the opposite. You're Treasure Travelers. You'll locate the artifacts and see that they get safely to their proper homes, such as museums or families they belong to."

"Who does the teapot belong to?" Allie asked.

"That one belongs to you," Juniper said. "Your parents can use it to pay for your furnace."

"This is so much." Vic looked overwhelmed as he paged through the book.

"Don't worry," Juniper said. "I'm going to teach you everything you need to know." She took a big breath. "The most

important thing to learn is how to keep away from Atlas."

"Oh!" Allie gasped. "I almost forgot about him. Why did he keep trying to steal Luna?"

"It wasn't Luna he was after,"

Juniper said. "It was the Infinity Spinner. He's been trying to collect them all since the end of time."

"Don't you mean the beginning of time?" Max asked.

"No. The end." Juniper reached into her red bag and pulled out three more Infinity Spinners. "These are for you. Keep them safe. He wants them for himself, but he doesn't know what you're all capable of."

"What are we capable of?" Allie asked.

"Oh, you'll see." Juniper winked. "We're just getting started."

WHAT'S AN
ANTIQUE STORE?

Allie and Vic spend a lot of time in Out of Time Antiques, their parents' shop in Philadelphia. The word *antiques* usually refers to things that are at least 100 years old. Along with silver tea sets, antique stores may sell everything from jewelry to furniture to old toys and photos.

Antique-store owners find items in a variety of places, including auctions and garage sales. They need to know a lot about history so they can figure out where each object came from and how much it is worth. Sometimes items aren't as old as they look!

ALL ABOARD:
TITANIC FACTS

Allie, Vic, and Max are amazed as Ruth shows them the Titanic's ballrooms, swimming pool, and other fancy features. Indeed, the real ship had a heated swimming pool, a gym full of exercise equipment, a barber shop, and beautiful restaurants that served lobster, caviar, and other fine foods.

Unfortunately, many of these things

were only for first-class passengers, so people with less money weren't allowed to use them. This was especially hard when it came to important things like crowded bedrooms and bathrooms, where hundreds of third-class passengers had to share two bathtubs.

For more facts, check out *Digging Up the Past: Titanic,* by Lisa J. Amstutz, on Epic!

WHO WERE MOLLY BROWN AND RUTH BECKER?

During their Titanic adventure, Allie, Vic, and Max meet Molly Brown, a wealthy woman who is more worried about her missing glove than the kids'

warnings that the ship could sink. Molly Brown was, in fact, a real person who helped other passengers board lifeboats and urged the crew on her own lifeboat to keep rescuing people as the ship sank. You can read more about Molly Brown in *Surviving a Shipwreck: The Titanic,* by Buffy Silverman, on Epic!

The kids also befriend Ruth, another real-life figure: Ruth Becker was only 12 years old when she boarded the Titanic with her mother, sister, and sick brother. Her family survived the disaster, and Ruth went on to become a teacher and have a family of her own. She lived until she was 90 years old.

About the Author

JESSICA RINKER is the author of *The Dare Sisters* as well as several picture book biographies. She teaches in the MFA program for Writing for Children and Young Adults at Sierra Nevada College and lives in West Virginia with her husband, who is also a children's author. If she could go back in time, she would choose to see her Viking ancestors building boats!

About the Illustrator

BETHANY STANCLIFFE is a central Washington–based artist who grew up in the Rockies, where she spent her time building tree forts, reading fairy tales, and filling up sketchbooks. Having had a spectrum of creative interests since childhood, she has found a home in illustration, where design and storytelling meet. Following in the footsteps of her parents, Bethany studied art and illustration at BYU-Idaho. She draws most of her inspiration from nature, films, and childhood adventures, and has a love for interesting textures and patterns. When she's not painting, she enjoys exploring outside with her son, Max, and creating original stories with her husband.

Out of Time: Lost on the Titanic

Text and illustrations copyright © 2020 by Epic! Creations, Inc. All rights reserved. Printed in China. No part of this book may be reproduced in any manner whatsoever without written permission except in the case of reprints in the context of reviews.

Andrews McMeel Publishing
a division of Andrews McMeel Universal
1130 Walnut Street, Kansas City, Missouri 64106

www.andrewsmcmeel.com

Epic! Creations, Inc.
702 Marshall Street, Suite 280, Redwood City, California 94063

20 21 22 23 24 SDB 10 9 8 7 6 5 4 3 2 1

Paperback ISBN: 978-1-5248-5825-4
Hardback ISBN: 978-1-5248-6043-1

Library of Congress Control Number: 2019956023

Photo credits: pages 1, 120–125, Paladin12/Shutterstock.com
page 121, Punkbarby0/Shutterstock.com
page 123, Everett Historical/Shutterstock.com
page 124, Everett Historical/Shutterstock.com

Design by Dan Nordskog

Made by:
King Yip (Dongguan) Printing & Packaging Factory Ltd.
Address and location of manufacturer:
Daning Administrative District, Humen Town
Dongguan Guangdong, China 523930
1st Printing—2/10/20

ATTENTION: SCHOOLS AND BUSINESSES
Andrews McMeel books are available at quantity discounts with bulk purchase for educational, business, or sales promotional use. For information, please e-mail the Andrews McMeel Publishing Special Sales Department: specialsales@amuniversal.com.